"It took me 17 years and 114 days to become an overnight success"

Leo Andrés Messi

SEAN WANTS TO BE
MESSI

By

TANYA PREMINGER

Illustrations

ELETTRA CUDIGNOTTO

To Sean, my light and my inspiration.

Contents

TANYA PREMINGER

13-5=?

Mummy and Sean sit at the kitchen table, working together on Sean's maths homework.

13-5=?

Sean looks at the numbers in his sloppy notebook and thinks, "Messi missed a kick yesterday against Réal Madrid!"

"Sean, thirteen minus five. How much is it?" Mummy taps her finger on the workbook page to bring Sean out of his daydream.

"Messi missed a kick! Can you believe it?!" Sean exclaims.

"Sean! Try to concentrate. That's enough football for right now."

"But how could Messi miss only 7 meters from the goal?"

Mummy reaches for the abacus that sits on the table and places it right in front of Sean.

"Thirteen minus five! Answer me, please!"

"Mummy, even so, Messi is the best football player ever!"

Mummy puts a hand to her forehead and sighs. At this rate, they will never get Sean's homework done!

Thoughtfully, Sean moves five beads on the abacus from left to right, one at a time. Mummy watches expectantly.

"Messi had five players guarding him, that's why! Even Messi can't score with such defence!" Sean concludes.

"Sean! The exercise!" Mummy yells, exasperated.

"Mummy, I don't need maths, I'm stupid. I'm going to be a football player." Sean smiles happily and sneaks a glance at the mirror on the back wall. He fixes his hair with his hand, picturing himself in a football stadium in front of the TV cameras.

Mummy closes her eyes. She takes a long breath.

"You are not stupid. Nobody is born with all the skills. They come with practise. Just like you practise football, you need to practise maths."

"Okay, okay," Sean says impatiently. "But you do remember that tomorrow you're signing me up for the football club, right?"

"Yes, I remember," Mummy smiles. "Are you sure you are not going to get scared? You don't know anyone there."

"So what?" Sean exclaims. "That's not a problem!"

First Visit to the Practise Field

"Sean, why did you drag me all the way here if you aren't going to get out of the car?" Mummy turns toward Sean, who is sitting in the backseat.

They are parked by the entrance to the training field. It's a good place to observe all the activity. Some parents drop off their children and drive away, while others escort them inside. Sean sees youngsters of all ages passing Mummy's car, dressed in the club's colourful uniforms, carrying their sports bags and footballs, and chatting excitedly on their way to class. A vendor stand is busy selling hot dogs, sweets, and snow-cones to the kids who have just finished a class.

Sean watches the scene and feels his stomach tighten up.

"Come on, Sean. Get out of the car already. Your practise starts now."

"No," Sean mumbles. "I want to go home." Despite what he told

5

Mummy yesterday, he feels very nervous.

"Oh, come on! Everyone is nervous the first time they try something new. There's nothing to be afraid of. I'm right here with you."

Mummy puts her handbag over one shoulder and Sean's gear bag over the other. She steps out of the car and opens the back door.

"Let's go!" she says sternly.

Sean backs away from her, clutching the handles of his booster seat and whimpering.

"I want to come back another time."

"We are not coming back another time!" Mummy yells. "I drove an hour just to bring you here! Come on and make the effort, Sean. You're acting spoiled!"

Mummy grabs Sean by the hand and tries to pull him out of the car, but he clings to the booster seat with all his might. Tears start running down his cheeks.

"Let's go home, Mummy…!"

Mummy sighs and shakes her head angrily.

"Fine. We'll go home. But I'm not wasting any more of my time on your football!"

Messi or Ronaldo?

During maths class at school, the class two kids sit quietly at their desks and write in their notebooks, practising multiplication as the teacher watches closely.

4 x 8 =?

Sean stares at the numbers, trying to concentrate. But, as usual, he is distracted by thoughts of football.

He steals a quick glance at his Messi book, which he has hidden inside his desk, then at his football, in its usual place by the door.

Michelle, the teacher's pet, approaches the teacher's desk and hands in her neat workbook page, first as always. The teacher examines it.

"Very good, Michelle," she says. "Everything is correct."

"Who else is finished and wants to show me his or her work?" the teacher asks, glancing at her watch. Around the room, other students begin to stand up with their finished work.

Sean looks at his empty worksheet. Then he leans toward Aidan, his best friend, who sits next to him, and whispers, "Manchester United wants to buy Messi from Barcelona for 500 million euro! Can you believe it?"

"Who cares?" sneers Aidan. "Messi stinks, Ronaldo rules!"

"Ronaldo is a loser!" Sean's voice rises in anger. "He misses an empty net!"

"Sean, quiet!" scolds the teacher. "You are disturbing everyone! I don't want to hear your voice again! This is your first and last warning."

"Okay, okay," mumbles Sean.

"Focus on your paper," the teacher continues. "You are going to be the last to hand your work in, once again."

I Want My Ball Back!

Joyful shouts can be heard all over the schoolyard. The playground and open field ring with the laughter of happy kids. At last, it is time for the break. Some kids chat excitedly with their friends, and others play on the playground equipment. More children play games in the open, grassy area beyond the swings. Sean, Aidan, and six other class two kids are in the heat of a football game.

Sean's face is already red, and sweat trickles through his hair as he dribbles the ball across the field. Two kids from the opposing team block his way. Sean expertly push-passes the ball to Aidan. Aidan receives it, advances, and passes one defender, but is stopped by another.

"Aidan! I'm open!" Sean yells. He stands in good position near the goal area. Aidan passes him the ball.

Just then, Hunter, a tall class six kid, charges onto the field uninvited. He tackles Sean aggressively, steals the ball from him, and shoots the ball into the net.

"Goooooooooal!" he calls, and runs to collect the ball.

"Not fair! You're interfering!" objects Aidan.

"You're not even playing with us!" calls Sean.

"Now I am," says Hunter, bouncing the ball on one foot, then on the other.

"Come on! Try to take the ball from me!" he teases.

Sean advances toward him nervously. Hunter waits until he gets nearer, then fakes Sean out, changes direction, and moves away. Sean tries to reach the ball, but Hunter keeps him at arm's length, juggling and shielding the ball from him. Hunter kicks the ball straight between Sean's open legs, then steals it from behind Sean's back. He snickers. So humiliating! Sean fights back his tears.

"It's my ball! Give it back!" Sean wails.

"Come get it," Hunter taunts.

Suddenly, the bell rings, signaling the end of the break. Hunter still has the ball. As he walks off the field, he kicks it forcefully over the fence and leaves, laughing all the while.

Sean runs around the fence to look for his ball, knowing he is going to be late for class.

Bedtime Story

That evening, Sean is in his football pyjamas, doing sit-ups on the living room couch. A football game is blaring from the telly, and Sean carefully observes the players' trick techniques. Just then, Daddy walks into the room.

"Oh, for goodness' sake. Turn off the telly already, Sean. It's time to go to bed."

"I'm not tired! The game just started!" whines Sean.

"I'm not going to say it again," Daddy answers firmly, searching for the remote.

Sean leaps toward the remote, which is hidden beneath his messy pile of football-player cards on the table, grabs it, and wedges it between himself and the back of the couch.

"Just until this game ends..." he pleads. "It's Barca against Valencia..."

"You have school tomorrow," Mummy interjects, entering the room and joining the conversation. "Off to bed you go!"

Daddy snatches the remote from Sean, and Sean pouts in disappointment.

"Then at least read me a bedtime story! I want a bedtime story!" he insists.

Mummy looks at Daddy and shrugs her shoulders.

"Okay. I suppose it's not too late for that," she says. "What do you want to read? The usual?"

Sean nods excitedly.

He runs upstairs and into the bathroom, where he washes his face and brushes his teeth quickly. Then he hops into bed, cradling his football. Mummy sits in a chair next to him, reading aloud from her tablet.

Sean bounces on the mattress and listens, staring dreamily at the posters and newspaper clips of Leo Messi that are plastered all over his walls.

Mummy reads: "Leo Messi, also known as 'The Atomic Flea', reached another milestone in his stellar footballing career over the weekend by scoring his 400th goal in an official competition for Barcelona... Stop jumping on the bed, Sean! I won't go on reading if you keep that up!"

"Go on, Mummy, I'm listening," Sean assures her as he continues to jump, still clutching his football.

"Despite being 27 years old," Mummy reads on, "the phenomenal forward has already amassed..." She pauses as Sean's pillow flies to the floor. "Sean! Stop it! I'm not reading if you can't sit still."

Mummy switches off her tablet and stands up to leave the room. Sean finally sits down.

"Mummy, I scored five goals yesterday when I was playing in the park with Daddy, and I score at least three times at school every day, so how many goals do I have in my career so far?"

Mummy just smiles.

"You see? If you listened in maths class, you could figure that out by yourself!" She kisses Sean goodnight and turns out the lights.

Practising with Daddy

Daddy and Sean play football in the park on Saturday evening. The sun is setting behind the trees, and shadows are dancing on their faces. Daddy dribbles toward the improvised goal. Sean tries his best to tackle him, but he slips, and Daddy scores.

"Goal!" Daddy calls triumphantly. Then he bends over, hands on his knees, and gasps for air. "Ten more minutes...and we go home..." he pants.

"No," objects Sean, "you've got to give me a chance to win!"

"This is the third time we've played this week..." Daddy catches his breath. "You need to start playing with kids your own age, like the kids in the football club. Why didn't you want to go to that?"

Sean shrugs his shoulders.

"Daddy, when you were small, and you played football on a team, did you get injured?" he asks, after a moment.

Daddy looks Sean over carefully. "Sometimes. It's a part of the game."

"Weren't you afraid?"

"Of course I was. But what can you do? If you want to be good at a sport, there are always risks."

"But those kids in the club are bigger than me," says Sean.

Daddy pats him on the shoulder. "They are your age. They are only bigger in size. And you'd better know this right now: there will always be somebody bigger and better than you. But when you play with better players, you learn twice as much."

Sean sighs despairingly and stares at the grass.

"Size is not what determines a good player," continues Daddy. "Good players think of ways to outsmart their opponents. They plan their attacks. They come up with different combinations of plays, and they try to do what others don't expect. Good players read a situation correctly and take advantage of it."

"Take advantage of a situation…" Sean contemplates this. "Does Messi do that, too?"

"Of course! Every good football player does it."

Sean is still thinking about this, when two younger kids arrive from the other side of the field. Their mother trails behind them.

"That's Justin. He's my friend. He lives around the corner from us," Sean tells Daddy, pointing to the taller of the two kids.

"Great. Why don't you see if he and his sister want to play football?" Daddy bends backwards and stretches his back, then pulls his phone out of his pocket. "I'll sit nearby," he says.

"They're too little. They don't know how to play football," Sean replies.

The kids approach timidly. Their mummy watches them from a bench.

"Hey, do you want to play football?" Daddy asks the kids.

They nod their heads.

"There you go, Sean. Teach them what you know. I bet you'd make a great coach." Daddy swipes a finger across the phone screen to wake it up.

"Okay, Daddy, you wait here. But you gotta watch me, so don't play with your phone."

Taking Advantage of a Situation

The training field buzzes with activity. The synthetic turf shines, lit by the powerful spotlights. Groups of kids of various ages practise football. Excitement fills the air.

Sean's age group is getting ready to start a game. Their trainer places small orange plastic cones on the artificial grass to mark the field and the goals. He counts the kids on each team and discovers he is missing one. He looks around.

Sean is standing at a safe distance, behind the full-sized portable metal goal. He's dressed in the club's uniform: high socks and shin guards and brand-new, colourful football cleats. He even has gel in his hair, Neymar style. Mummy stands next to him, holding his new gear bag.

The trainer yells in Sean's direction, "Hey, new boy! Are you here to play?"

Sean does not answer. He turns his back to him and looks frantically at Mummy.

"Go play, Sean," Mummy urges. Sean shakes his head in fearful refusal.

The trainer raises his voice. "What's your name, boy? Come on; we're missing a player."

The other kids are waiting, all eyes on Sean, but Sean lowers his gaze and clings to Mummy.

"His name is Sean," Mummy replies. "Go on, Sean, go play." She gives him a gentle push toward the group.

Sean resists and backs away from her. He tightly hugs the pole of the goal. Mummy raises her hands in a helpless gesture.

"Okay, he can join later." The trainer shrugs his shoulders and turns to the group of players. Moving to the center of the field, he delivers a high kickoff to start the game. Mummy and Sean watch as the kids struggle to get possession of the ball and form an attack.

"Sean, I don't know why I'm paying for this class if you won't participate!" Mummy exclaims, annoyed.

Sean keeps quiet.

"You have to get over your fear, Sean. Come on, I'm here with you. What's so scary about this?"

"I don't feel well." Sean wipes a tear from his eye.

Loud cheers echo across the field as one group scores a goal.

"Sean," pleads Mummy, "I know that it's hard, but everybody's afraid sometimes. Even grownups. The key is to overcome your fear."

"I want to go home." Tears are running down Sean's cheeks now.

"If you don't try, you'll never be like Messi!" Mummy looks Sean in the eye with disappointment.

"I don't want to be like Messi" Sean mumbles stubbornly, scuffing his football cleats on the ground.

Excited cries ring out once again, as a boy manages to get through the defence and advances toward his opponent's goal. Just when the situation seems hopeless for the other team, a big boy with a Mohawk haircut charges at the other boy and slide-tackles him. The boy loses his balance, rolls over, and scrapes his knees badly. The trainer runs in and stops the game.

Everybody else approaches to assess the situation. The injured boy is howling with pain.

"Foul! Foul play!" he cries. "He slide-tackled me!"

Mummy looks at Sean. "Sean! It's your chance. You can join the game now!"

"I don't want to play," Sean insists, crossing his arms.

The trainer calms the injured boy and helps him off the field.

"Hey, Sean, do you want to join us now?" he calls.

Sean does not answer. He pouts and shrugs his shoulders.

"I'll buy you a pack of football cards if you get in and play," Mummy offers desperately.

Sean sniffs back his tears and wipes his face with his sleeve.

"The fancy hologram ones…" Mummy adds.

Sean considers this for another second.

"Two packs," he says.

Mummy raises her eyebrows, then sighs. "Agreed."

Sean runs timidly onto the field. He feels his stomach knot with anxiety.

"Go, Sean!" the trainer cheers.

The players align in the center of the field, and the trainer kicks off.

While the other kids run after the ball, trying frantically to seize it from one another, Sean keeps away from it. He stands apart from the group, occasionally moving onto the opponent's part of the field and back again. The other kids don't initiate many passes. Each player who takes possession of the ball tries to score by himself, so Sean is easily overlooked by his teammates.

In the next ten minutes, the opposing team scores two goals. Sean hasn't even touched the ball yet. He stands at the corner of

the field, watching Mummy with guilty eyes.

The leader of Sean's team gets the ball and breaks into the opposing team's territory. All the defenders surround him so he doesn't have a line on the goal. Seeing that he is going to lose the ball, he quickly passes to Sean, who stands by himself, away from everybody. Surprised, Sean receives the ball and dribbles it toward the goal. As the goalie runs at him, Sean slides the ball past his left side. The ball flies speedily into the net.

It's a goal!

"Goooooooooooooooal! Hurray!" yells Mummy.

"Go, Sean!" hollers the trainer.

Sean's teammates surround him, hugging him and giving him high-fives. Sean smiles timidly and glances over at Mummy.

Throughout the rest of the game, Sean maintains the same tactic. By the time the trainer blows his whistle to mark the end of the game, Sean has scored two more times. As the players disperse, Sean approaches Mummy, beaming with pleasure.

"Mummy, did you see me score? I made three goals!" he cheers. "And I also took advantage of a situation!"

A House in
Paris Saint-Germain

The next evening, Sean and Mummy sit at the kitchen table with Sean's maths workbook. Sean is wearing one of his Messi jerseys, number 10, with his high socks and cleats. His new packs of football hologram cards are spread on the table close by.

"Well, Sean, 80-67= how much?" asks Mummy.

"Mummy," interrupts Sean, "how many seasons does a professional football player need to play if he wants to buy a house?"

"Well, that depends on the house," smiles Mummy. "And on how much the player earns each season."

Sean thinks for a moment.

"Let's say a player earns 50 million euro for a season," he says thoughtfully. "After five seasons, he would have 250 million. Is that enough for a house?"

"I believe so."

"If I were him, I would buy one house in Barcelona, one in Brazil, and one house in Paris Saint-Germain just for you, Mummy."

"That is some smart thinking," Mummy says happily. "Did you notice that you just solved a complicated maths problem? Looks like you've scored once again!"

END OF BOOK 1

To be continued...

To get the next book and to check out
the personalization service, go to:
sean-wants-to-be-messi.com

22393602R00022

Printed in Great Britain
by Amazon